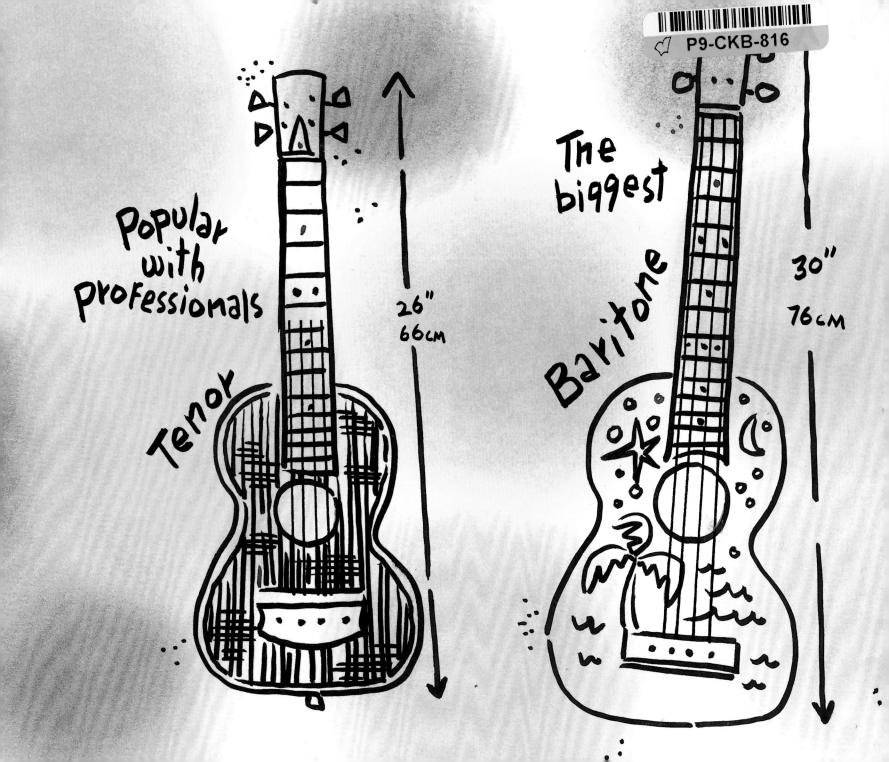

Popular with Professionals

Tenor

26"
66CM

The biggest

Baritone

30"
76CM

My Dog Has FLEAS!

A Ukulele Misadventure

Bob Barner

HOLIDAY HOUSE • NEW YORK

To Carolyn Hui, ukulele teacher extraordinaire and fearless leader of the Dolphin Ukulele Club.

Library of Congress Cataloging-in-Publication Data
Names: Barner, Bob, author.
Title: My dog has fleas! / Bob Barner.
Description: First edition. | New York : Holiday House, 2021. | Includes a history of the ukulele as well as the song and chords "My Dog has Fleas" that was the inspiration for this book. | Audience: Ages 4–8.
Audience: Grades K–1. | Summary: A pack of flea infested pups flees from their bath, but a song on the ukulele might just bring them back.
Identifiers: LCCN 2020020190 | ISBN 9780823446421 (hardcover)
Subjects: CYAC: Stories in rhyme. | Dogs—Fiction. | Ukulele—Fiction. Fleas—Fiction.
Classification: LCC PZ8.3.B252425 My 2021 | DDC [E]—dc23
LC record available at https://lccn.loc.gov/2020020190
ISBN: 978-0-8234-4642-1 (hardcover)

MY DOG HAS FLEAS

Bob Barner
Inspired by Twinkle, Twinkle

MY DOG HAS FLEAS is a handy melody that helps us tune a ukulele. When the strings of a ukulele make the proper sound, it's called being in tune, or making the correct musical sound. When you sing MY DOG HAS FLEAS with the ukulele in tune, it will help you remember the sounds the ukulele strings should make.

Start with the string closest to your chin.
G string: sing "My."
C string: sing "dog."
E string: sing "has."
A string: sing "fleas."
MY DOG HAS FLEAS is also the inspiration for this book.

I play ukulele and my dog sings along.
Her friends all wag to a rocking song.

Pups look itchy by the shady trees.
Chew! Chew! Chew! My dog has fleas!

Maurice

Ava

Lucy

Sophie

Mila

Oliver

Spotty

Bear

My
Dog

We run up hills and down the trails,
grabbing at leashes and zigzagging tails.

I beg my pooch, stop running please.
Woof! Woof! Woof! My dog has fleas!

We strum the ukes to call them back.
My shaggy dog is leader of the pack!

Race by trucks, sniff whiffs of cheese.
Sniff! Sniff! Sniff! My dog has fleas!

Her pack zips through a picnic spread.
Juice goes flying with cookies and bread.

They bolt away to the dogwood trees.
It's a woofing mess. My dog has fleas!

Splashing in a pond with croaking frogs.
They're a panting pack of hairy wet dogs.

Worn-out hounds are caught with ease.
Time for baths. My dog has fleas!

I scrub fuzzy tails, snouts, and ears.
We wash fleas off their scruffy rears.

With one big shake on wobbly knees
her fleas are gone. My dog had fleas!

I play ukulele and we all sing along.
"My dog had fleas!" is a favorite song.

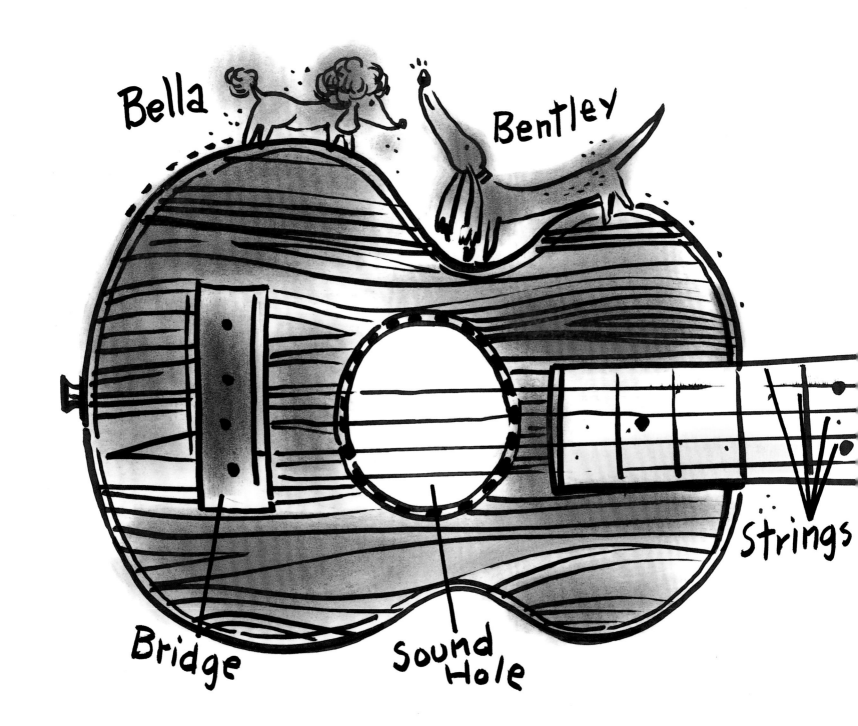

UKULELE HISTORY

Jumping Fleas! Does your dog have fleas?

Some people claim that the fingers of ukulele players move so quickly that it looks like little fleas jumping. The word ukulele may come from joining *uku* (meaning "flea") and *lele* (meaning "jump"). Jumping flea. Another story says it means a "gift to come."

The ukulele story starts with a British clipper ship named the S.S. *Ravenscrag* that sailed from Portugal to Honolulu, Hawaii, in 1879. When it finally arrived at Honolulu, João Fernandes disembarked and entertained the locals with songs played on his small guitar-like instrument called a machete or a braguinha. Manuel Nunes, Augusto Dias, and Jose do Espirito Santo were among the passengers aboard for the four-month trip. They worked at sugar plantations but eventually became ukulele makers and sold them in music shops. With time

the instrument was modified and developed into the ukulele we know today. King David Kalākaua enjoyed ukulele music and had it performed at many royal events. The king learned to play the ukulele and helped make it popular in Hawaii. After the king, Queen Lili'uokalani was also musical and wrote two hundred songs including the very well-known "Aloha 'Oe."

Thousands of Americans first heard ukulele music at the 1915 Panama Pacific International Exposition held in San Francisco. The Hawaiian Pavilion featured a guitar and ukulele band.

Ukuleles are usually made of wood, but some are made of plastic. More expensive ukuleles are made of hardwoods like mahogany. A favorite wood for ukuleles is koa, which is grown in Hawaii. Most ukuleles have a figure-eight body, others are oval, or pineapple shaped. Some are square or made out of a wooden cigar box.

People all over the world play ukuleles. They are most popular in the United States, Japan, Canada, England, Australia, Hawaii, and Europe. Israel Kamakawiwo'ole or 'Iz' and Jake Shimabukuro are talented ukulele players you might enjoy.

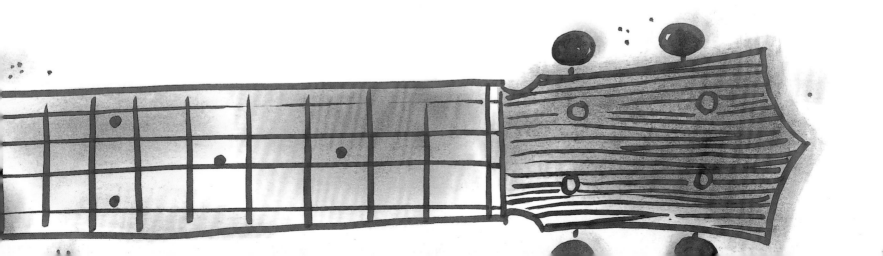

THE SONG AND CHORDS

C CHORD

Fret 1.
Fret 2.
Fret 3.

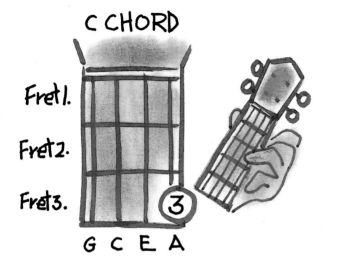

G C E A

F CHORD

G C E A

G CHORD

G C E A

If you want to play the ukulele, these drawings will help you get started.

The chord drawings show where to put your fingers on the strings to make the right sounds.

Press the strings down between the frets with your fingertips and strum the strings with the thumb on the other hand. The easiest way to make sure the ukulele is in tune is to use a ukulele tuner or a piano.

The strings are tuned to G, C, E and A. The G string is closest to your chin. The A string is closest to the floor. The numbers in the circles show where to place your fingers on the ukulele fretboard.

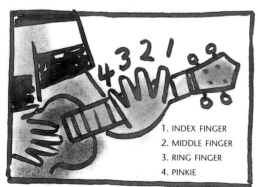

1. INDEX FINGER
2. MIDDLE FINGER
3. RING FINGER
4. PINKIE

Fingers are numbered on the chord drawings to show where they go on the ukulele.

You can sit or stand to play the ukulele. Hold it like this when you stand.

Rest it on your lap when you sit. Place your thumb on the back of the neck while playing.